For Mum, Jacob and my expanding family,
your support has been invaluable to me.

For Ian, Delilah and Cece,
my precious snowflakes.

First published, November 2022

Text copyright © Jessica Holme 2022

Illustrations copyright © Georgia Coote 2022

High in the sky,
in a full bloom cloud,
was a sad snowflake.

Jacob was only a very
little snowflake.
More like a crystal...

...small and precious.

"What an earth is the matter?" asked his mother when she found him huddled in the cloud.

"I don't want to be a snowflake" said Jacob with a little sniff, snuggling further into the cloud.

"Why not?" said his mother, "It is wonderful to be a snowflake. Look at how perfect you are becoming. You will be the brightest snowflake in the cloud."

Jacob looked puzzled; he was so small.
How could he be unique?

"But soon," he argued, "I'll grow heavy and I'll have to leave the cloud."

His mother nodded. "I don't want to be a snowflake," he repeated.

"Come now," cooed his mother, "leaving the cloud is the most wonderful adventure of all."

"How do you know?" said Jacob,
"you've not left the cloud yet."

"Well," said his mother, pausing,
"think how many snowflakes leave
the cloud, they wouldn't all do it
unless it was an adventure."

Jacob thought about this, he thought a lot.

He thought so hard that his thoughts became their own things. Bigger and bolder than he.

His thoughts made him want to hide further into the cloud where the other snowflakes were. He tried his utmost to be part of the cloud, safe and comfortable with those around him.

But time will always win its game of hide and seek.

Eventually, it was Jacob's turn to leave the cloud, he could feel it. He was big and heavy and ready to follow his friends and family on the big adventure.

Jacob breathed a deep breath for there was nothing left for him to do.

As he dropped, he felt weightless and completely free. There was just so much space around him. Yet when he looked around, he was not alone... there were lots of snowflakes.

His mother had been right,
it was an adventure.

A strong wind led them into a spiralling dance. Smiling and laughing, they went with the wind, following its twists and turns.

The beauty of it all never stop amazing him. He wished everyone in the cloud could know just how beautiful it all was. How the spirals made by others created beauty in the sky.

Some gusts were stronger than others and it felt like it would shake him till he'd break into a thousand tiny shards. He would try to move out of the winds path, but its hands were too wide and its grip too strong. The only thing the Jacob could do was breathe and watch his friends' shimmer in the light.

Like all great adventures,
Jacob only had to be brave
for as long as he was able.

The same wind which
had blown them sideways
and down, lifted them up
in a gentle embrace.
It felt wonderful.
Truly wonderful.

After what seemed an eternity,
Jacob landed on something soft,
warm and comforting. Jacob
looked up and saw what a long
way he had come. He rested
there peacefully.

He loved being

a snowflake

Some questions for after reading 'I don't want to be a snowflake!'

Can you find Jacob in the story?

What makes you unique?

Has there been a time when you felt nervous?

What helps you when dealing with change?

Take one breath now and imagine you're floating like Jacob the snowflake, how does that feel?

Printed in Great Britain
by Amazon

11490463R00016